Bill's Scary Backpack

by Susan Gates

Illustrated by Anni Axworthy

FRANKLIN WATTS
LONDON • SYDNEY

First published in 2010 by
Franklin Watts
338 Euston Road
London
NW1 3BH

Franklin Watts Australia
Level 17/207 Kent Street
Sydney
NSW 2000

Text © Susan Gates 2010
Illustration © Anni Axworthy 2010

A CIP catalogue record for this book is available
from the British Library.

ISBN 978 0 7496 9458 6 (hbk)
ISBN 978 0 7496 9468 5 (pbk)

Series Editor: Jackie Hamley
Series Advisor: Catherine Glavina
Series Designer: Peter Scoulding

Printed in China

Franklin Watts is a divison of
Hachette Children's Books,
an Hachette UK company.
www.hachette.co.uk

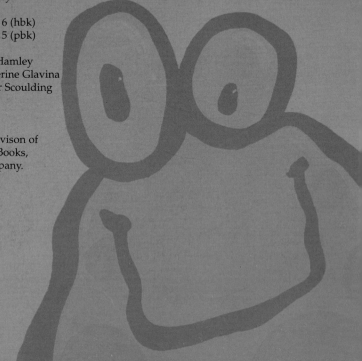

Bill opened his birthday present.

A scary face stared
up at him.

It had spiky hair, big sharp teeth, a long red tongue and goggly eyes on springs.

"It's a monster!"
said Bill, leaping away.

"No," laughed Mum. "Look!
It's a new backpack."
"Cool!" said Bill.

Bill wore his backpack to school. On the walk there, he played with his new yoyo. He soon forgot about the backpack.

Bill walked past a little girl.
"Help!" she yelled,
and ran away.

Bill stared after her.
"What's the matter
with her?" he said.

Bill walked past a baby
in a pram.

"Waaaa!" cried the baby, pulling up her blanket.

"You scared my baby!"
shouted the baby's mum.

"Me?" said Bill.

"But I didn't do anything!"

Bill walked on.

A cat hissed and
ran under a bush.

Bill walked into the park.

A fierce dog was chasing a little boy.

The dog saw Bill.

It raced away.

"Thanks!" said the boy.
"You really scared that
horrible dog!"

"I don't get it," said Bill,
shaking his head.
"Why am I so scary?"

"It's not you. It's your backpack," grinned the boy.

Suddenly Bill grinned too.
"I forgot that!" said Bill.

"So that's why I'm
so scary!"

Puzzle 1

a

b

c

d

e

f

Put these pictures in the correct order.
Now tell the story in your own words.
How short can you make the story?

confused   upset

excited

grateful   glum

pleased

Choose the words which best describe each character. Can you think of any more? Pretend to be one of the characters!

Answers

Puzzle 1

The correct order is:

1d, 2a, 3e, 4c, 5f, 6b

Puzzle 2

Bill   The correct word is confused.

The incorrect words are excited, upset.

Boy   The correct words are grateful, pleased.

The incorrect word is glum.

Look out for more Leapfrog stories:

The Little Star
ISBN 978 0 7496 3833 7

Mary and the Fairy
ISBN 978 0 7496 9142 4

Jack's Party
ISBN 978 0 7496 4389 8

Pippa and Poppa
ISBN 978 0 7496 9140 0

The Bossy Cockerel
ISBN 978 0 7496 9141 7

The Best Snowman
ISBN 978 0 7496 9143 1

Big Bad Blob
ISBN 978 0 7496 7092 4*
ISBN 978 0 7496 7796 1

Cara's Breakfast
ISBN 978 0 7496 7797 8

Croc's Tooth
ISBN 978 0 7496 7799 2

The Magic Word
ISBN 978 0 7496 7800 5

Tim's Tent
ISBN 978 0 7496 7801 2

Why Not?
ISBN 978 0 7496 7798 5

Sticky Vickie
ISBN 978 0 7496 7986 6

Handyman Doug
ISBN 978 0 7496 7987 3

Billy and the Wizard
ISBN 978 0 7496 7985 9

Sam's Spots
ISBN 978 0 7496 7984 2

Bill's Baggy Trousers
ISBN 978 0 7496 3829 0

Bill's Bouncy Shoes
ISBN 978 0 7496 7990 3

Bill's Scary Backpack
ISBN 978 0 7496 9458 6*
ISBN 978 0 7496 9468 5

Little Joe's Big Race
ISBN 978 0 7496 3832 0

Little Joe's Balloon Race
ISBN 978 0 7496 7989 7

Little Joe's Boat Race
ISBN 978 0 7496 9457 9*
ISBN 978 0 7496 9467 8

Felix on the Move
ISBN 978 0 7496 4387 4

Felix and the Kitten
ISBN 978 0 7496 7988 0

Felix Takes the Blame
ISBN 978 0 7496 9456 2*
ISBN 978 0 7496 9466 1

The Cheeky Monkey
ISBN 978 0 7496 3830 6

Cheeky Monkey on Holiday
ISBN 978 0 7496 7991 0

Cheeky Monkey's Treasure Hunt
ISBN 978 0 7496 9455 5*
ISBN 978 0 7496 9465 4

For details of all our titles go to: www.franklinwatts.co.uk

*hardback